THE DRAGON HALLOWEEN PARTY

THE DRAGON HALLOWEEN PARTY

WRITTEN AND ILLUSTRATED BY

LOREEN LEEDY

HOLIDAY HOUSE · NEW YORK

Library of Congress Cataloging-in-Publication Data

Leedy, Loreen.
The dragon Halloween party.

Summary: The dragons prepare a Halloween party
complete with costumes, decorations,
and appropriate food and activities.
    [1. Halloween—Fiction.   2. Dragons—Fiction.
3. Parties—Fiction.   4. Stories in rhyme]   I. Title.
PZ8.3.L4995Dt   1986   [E]   86-286
ISBN 0-8234-0611-3

for KAREN

"Halloween is coming soon,"
Ma Dragon yells one afternoon.
"Let's all plan to celebrate,
We'll cook and clean and decorate.

"Think of what you want to be—
A wizard, clown, or bumblebee,
Perhaps a pirate or a king,
You can be most anything!"

8

Each dragon snips and clips with care
To make a costume he can wear.

CROWN 1. On construction paper or poster board, draw a crown and cut out.

2. Tape ends together so crown fits head.

3. Using glue, decorate with buttons, beads, sequins or jewels.

SCEPTER 1. Cut out two diamond shapes from construction paper or poster board.

2. Glue diamond shapes together with wooden stick in between.

3. Using glue, decorate with sequins, beads, and glitter.

CLOWN HAT 1. Roll construction paper into cone shape to fit head.

2. Tape cone. Trim excess paper.

3. Cut circles from colorful paper and glue to hat. Glue pom-pom on top.

4. Glue two ribbons to inside of hat.

WIZARD HAT Decorate with moon and star shapes. **WAND** Follow directions for scepter, but cut out two star shapes. Decorate with glue and glitter.

SUPER HERO MASK 1. On poster board, draw and cut out mask.

2. Carefully cut out slits for eyes.

3. Glue on ribbons and feathers.

CRYSTAL BALL AND FORTUNE TELLER 1. Cut strip of construction paper for base.

2. Put glue around edge and set plastic ball on base.

3. Paint ball with glow-in-the-dark paint.

4. Wear scarves and jewelry to complete outfit.

BUTTERFLY WINGS
1. On poster board, draw wings, and cut out.

2. Using glue, decorate the outside with sequins, paper cutouts and glitter.

3. Glue four ribbons to inside.

FEELERS
1. Cut out paper strip.

2. Tape ends together to fit head.

3. Curl ends of two pipe cleaners and glue to inside. Secure with tape.

MONSTER 1. Put brown paper bag over head. Feel for eyes and lightly mark with pencil.

2. Cut out eyes. If necessary, trim "shoulders" to fit.

3. Make features with paper cutouts, crayons or markers.

4. Glue paper claws to old gloves.

PIRATE HAT 1. Cut out two hat shapes from poster board or construction paper. Glue edges together, leaving bottom open.

2. Cut two bones from white paper. Glue to hat.

SWORD 1. Cut out sword from cardboard.

2. Paint gold or silver.

EYE PATCH Cut two circles from black felt. Sandwich string or elastic between circles and glue to hold.

BUMBLEBEE 1. On poster board, draw two body-sized ovals and cut out.

2. With black marker, draw stripes on both sides.

3. Cut white paper wings and black stinger. Glue to back.

4. Glue four ribbons to the inside of each oval.

5. Make feelers (see page 11) and glue pom-pom to ends.

**FAIRY PRINCESS
1.** Tie a sash around waist.

2. Tuck a scarf around sash.

3. Keep adding scarves to complete skirt.

4. Make small wings, crown, and wand (see pages 10-11) to complete costume.

CAPE 1. Use any piece of cloth. Fold top to inside as shown.

2. Fasten at neck with safety pin.

3. Fold down collar.

4. Cape may be decorated with paint, or glued-on cutouts.

The dragons draw and cut and glue
Bats and ghosts and spiders, too.

BAT GARLAND
1. Use a strip of black paper.

2. Fold paper accordian-style.

3. Draw bat and cut out, leaving wing tips uncut.

4. Unfold bats.

5. Repeat and tape sections together to make one long garland.

GHOSTS 1. Unfold two tissues.

2. Overlap the two tissues.

3. Crumple a third tissue into a ball and place as shown.

4. Twist tissues around ball to form neck.

5. Tie thread around neck.

6. Thread a needle and push through top of ghost's head. Remove needle.

7. Draw face with marker. Use tape or thumbtack to hang.

SPIDERS 1. Twist four pipe cleaners together.

2. Spread out to form eight legs.

3. Tie thread around legs. Thread one end of thread through needle. Push needle through pom-pom. Remove needle.

4. Apply drop of glue and push pom-pom into place.

5. Use tape or thumbtack to hang.

13

With creepy monsters hung in space,
The cave becomes a spooky place.

GIANT PAPER MONSTER

1. On separate pieces of paper, draw and color the parts of a monster.

2. Cut out each part.

3. Glue parts together.

4. Hang monster on wall with tape or thumbtacks.

14

Ma takes a spoon and carving knife
And makes the pumpkins come to life.

Cut hole in top

Scoop out pulp

Draw face

Cut out features

Put candle or
flashlight inside

15

By putting food in wacky places,
The dragons make some funny faces.

Green pepper head, strawberry nose,
olive eyes, green bean mouth

Cabbage head, carrot nose and horns,
prune eyes, cheese teeth

Use toothpicks to hold features in place.

Eggplant head, marshmallow eyeballs,
raisin pupils, gumdrop mouth,
cherry tomato nose, leaf hair

Large apple head, grape eyes,
mushroom cap nose, lettuce hair,
orange peel mouth

Pumpkin Ice Cream Squares

Place 8 to 10 ginger cookies (see p. 18) into a plastic bag and crush with rolling pin. Sprinkle crumbs on bottom of 9" X 13" X 2" pan.

Mix— 2 c. canned pumpkin
1 tsp. pumpkin pie spice

Add— ½ gallon slightly softened vanilla ice cream.

Mix thoroughly and pour into pan.

Chop ⅔ c. pecans and sprinkle on top of ice cream. Freeze for at least four hours. Cut into squares and serve promptly.

Everyone will want a treat
Of something cold and something sweet.

17

Ginger cookies spiced just right . . .

GINGER° COOKIES
Preheat oven to 350° F
Cream— ½ c. shortening
        ¾ c. sugar
Add— 1 egg
      ¼ c. molasses
      1 tbs. vinegar
Sift— 2 c. flour
       ¼ tsp. salt
       1 tsp. baking soda
       1 tsp. ginger
       ¼ tsp. cinnamon
Add to egg mixture.
Drop spoonfuls of dough onto greased
cookie sheet. Bake 12-14 minutes.
Makes 5 dozen two-inch cookies.

And witch's brew by candlelight.

WITCH'S BREW
Pour one gallon apple cider into saucepan. Add eight whole cloves and an orange cut into quarters. Heat well (but don't boil) and serve.

The moon is up, it's getting late,
It's almost time to celebrate!

All the guests come running in.
At last the party can begin.

Ma relates a scary tale,
A little dragon starts to wail.

25

They pin a hat upon a witch,
The numbers show whose hat is which.

They bob for apples, dance and swing,
Run in circles, laugh and sing.

When the guests go home, they cry,
"Happy Halloween! Good-bye!"

31

A Dragon Costume For You

HEAD

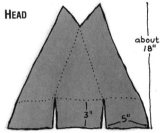 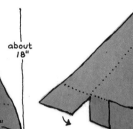 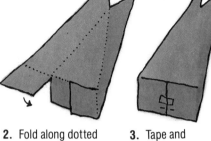  

1. Draw head shape on poster board. Cut out, then cut slits.

2. Fold along dotted lines as shown.

3. Tape and staple tabs.

4. Tape and staple nose.

5. Glue on two pom-poms, then two green felt irises. Glue two poster board eyebrows to back of eyeballs.

6. Cut and tape two paper teeth. Draw nostrils, mouth and pupils with black marker. Glue ribbon ties to inside.

BODY

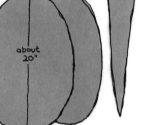 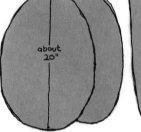 

2. Tape tail to back oval. Glue on dark pink paper stripes. Trim excess.

3. Cut, crease, and glue five paper triangles down middle of back.

1. Draw two ovals and one tail on blue poster board and cut out.

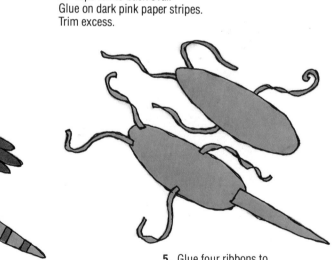 

4. Cut two wings from purple paper. Glue to body.

5. Glue four ribbons to each oval, at "shoulders" and "waist."

6. Wear blue clothing under costume. Tie head ribbons under chin. Tie front to back at shoulders and waist.

"Hey!" a loud voice said. "Why are you hanging upside down?"

Stellaluna's eyes opened wide. She saw a most peculiar face. "I'm not upside down, *you* are!" Stellaluna said.

"Ah, but you're a *bat*. Bats hang by their feet. You are hanging by your thumbs, so that makes you *upside down!*" the creature said. "I'm a bat. I am hanging by my feet. That makes me *right side up!*"

Stellaluna was confused. "Mama Bird told me I was upside down. She said I was wrong . . ."

"Wrong for a bird, maybe, but not for a bat."

More bats gathered around to see the strange young bat who behaved like a bird. Stellaluna told them her story.

"You ate *b-bugs?*" stuttered one.

"You slept at *night?*" gasped another.

"How very strange," they all murmured.

"Wait! Wait! Let me look at this child." A bat pushed through the crowd. "An *owl* attacked you?" she asked. Sniffing Stellaluna's fur, she whispered, "You are *Stellaluna*. You are my baby."

"You escaped the owl?" cried Stellaluna. "You survived?"

"Yes," said Mother Bat as she wrapped her wings around Stellaluna. "Come with me and I'll show you where to find the most delicious fruit. You'll never have to eat another bug as long as you live."

"But it's nighttime," Stellaluna squeaked. "We can't fly in the dark or we will crash into trees."

"We're bats," said Mother Bat. "We can see in darkness. Come with us."

Stellaluna was afraid, but she let go of the tree and dropped into the deep blue sky.

Stellaluna *could* see. She felt as though rays of light shone from her eyes. She was able to see everything in her path.

Soon the bats found a mango tree, and Stellaluna ate as much of the fruit as she could hold.

"I'll never eat another bug as long as I live," cheered Stellaluna as she stuffed herself full. "I must tell Pip, Flitter, and Flap!"

The next day Stellaluna went to visit the birds.

"Come with me and meet my bat family," said Stellaluna.

"Okay, let's go," agreed Pip.

"They hang by their feet and they fly at night and they eat the best food in the world," Stellaluna explained to the birds on the way.

As the birds flew among the bats, Flap said, "I feel upside down here."

So the birds hung by their feet.

"Wait until dark," Stellaluna said excitedly. "We will fly at night."

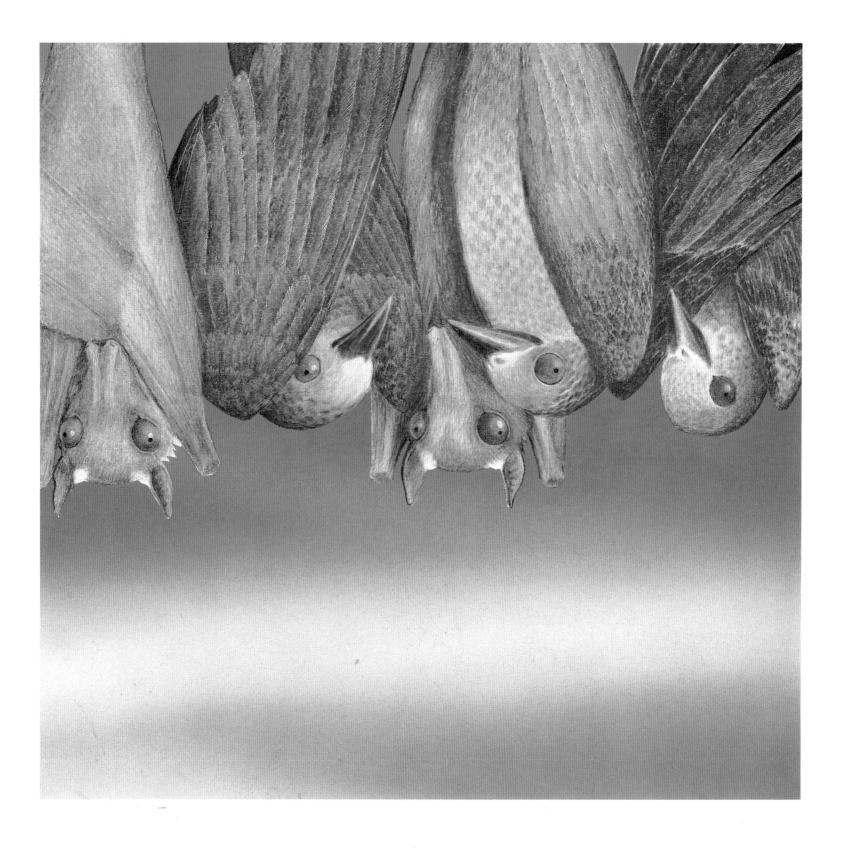

When night came Stellaluna flew away. Pip, Flitter, and Flap leapt from the tree to follow her.

"I can't see a thing!" yelled Pip.

"Neither can I," howled Flitter.

"Aaeee!" shrieked Flap.

"They're going to crash," gasped Stellaluna. "I must rescue them!"

Stellaluna swooped about, grabbing her friends in the air. She lifted them to a tree, and the birds grasped a branch. Stellaluna hung from the limb above them.

"We're safe," said Stellaluna. Then she sighed. "I wish you could see in the dark, too."

"We wish you could land on your feet," Flitter replied. Pip and Flap nodded.

They perched in silence for a long time.

"How can we be so different and feel so much alike?" mused Flitter.

"And how can we feel so different and be so much alike?" wondered Pip.

"I think this is quite a mystery," Flap chirped.

"I agree," said Stellaluna. "But we're friends. And that's a fact."

BAT NOTES

Of the nearly 4,000 species of mammals on Earth, almost one quarter are bats, the only mammals capable of powered flight.

The scientific name for bats is Chiroptera, "hand-wing," because the skeleton that supports the wing is composed of the animal's elongated finger bones.

The majority of bats are classified as Microchiroptera, "small hand-wing." Nearly 800 varieties fill special niches in every climate around the world except the polar zones. The lifestyles and food preferences of Microchiroptera vary widely. Many eat insects, while others catch fish, amphibians, and reptiles. Finally, there is the famous vampire, of which there are only three species, ranging from Mexico to Argentina. The vampire's victims are mostly domestic cattle and native mammals and birds.

The other 170 or so species of bats are the fruit bats, otherwise known as Megachiroptera, or "large hand-wing." As their name implies, these are the largest bats, some types boasting wingspans of six feet.

Fruit bats generally have long muzzles, large eyes, pointy ears, and furry bodies, which is why they are often called flying foxes. Unlike the Microchiroptera, who travel by echolocation, fruit bats depend on their keen vision and sense of smell to navigate. They live in tropical and subtropical climates that provide year-round supplies of their favorite fruit, flowers, and nectar. Some fruit bats, as they forage for nectar, are responsible for pollination of many types of night-blooming trees and plants. Others eat whole fruits, seeds and all, and distribute the seeds over the forest floor in their droppings. Regeneration of tropical forests depends greatly on bats.

The illustrations in this book were done in Liquitex acrylics
and Prismacolor pencils on bristol board.
The display type was hand-lettered by Judythe Sieck.
The text type was set in Guardi #55 by Thompson Type, San Diego, California.
Color separations by Bright Arts, Ltd., Singapore
Printed and bound by Tien Wah Press, Singapore
Production supervision by Warren Wallerstein and Ginger Boyer
Designed by Trina Stahl